Cinderella's

By Alexis Barad

Illustrated by Atelier Philippe Harchy

Random House 🏠 New York

Copyright © 2005 Disney Enterprises, Inc. All rights reserved under International and Pan-American Copyright Conventions. Published in the United States by Random House Children's Books, a division of Random House, Inc., New York, NY 10019, and simultaneously in Canada by Random House of Canada Limited, Toronto, in conjunction with Disney Enterprises, Inc. RANDOM HOUSE and colophon are registered trademarks of Random House, Inc.

Library of Congress Control Number: 2004093751   ISBN: 0-7364-2325-7

www.randomhouse.com/kids/disney

MANUFACTURED IN CHINA

10 9 8 7 6 5 4 3 2

$\mathcal{A}$re you good at keeping secrets? I hope you
are, because I have a secret that no one knows—
well, no one human, that is: I have a hiding place
way up high in the castle attic.

Now that I'm married to the Prince, I am
always busy going to fancy parties, planning
banquets, and learning how to act like royalty.
Who knew being a princess could be such
hard work?

Luckily, I found a place I can escape to
when I need a break from my Princess duties
and want to be with my dearest little friends.
The best part is that it's my very own secret
hiding spot!

I have lots of parties in my secret room.
The mice and I share tea while they tell me
all the news from the village. Once, Suzy told
me that the butcher had fallen in love with
the tavern keeper's daughter. They were
planning a beautiful garden wedding!

Gus loves to hear about the royal banquets I attend. I tell him stories about dining with kings and queens and how we use a different fork for every course—sometimes I eat with eight forks during one meal! Of course, talking about food always makes Gus hungry.

I keep my trunk of treasures in my secret
hiding place. It's filled with my favorite
books, beautiful fabrics, and keepsakes from
my mother. Even the glass slipper that led me
to marry the Prince is safely tucked away in
my trunk.

I keep a scrapbook in my secret place, too!
I fill it with pressed flowers from the castle
grounds, love letters from the Prince, and
funny pictures that Suzy likes to draw of me
and our friends.

Sometimes we eat cookies that I make from
my mother's old recipe book. We share them
with the birds on the window ledge. They
wouldn't let out a peep about my secret place!

Once, when I wasn't there, Pom-Pom, the
castle's cat, found her way to my hidden
staircase and almost made it to the attic.
Luckily, the mice heard her. They sent one of
the birds to get my dog, Bruno, quickly!

Bruno charged up the stairs and chased Pom-Pom back down. That was a close one! I would hate it if anyone found my secret hiding spot!

The mice love to play dress-up, and my hiding spot is the perfect place for it. I make them little costumes to laugh and play in. When I tell them funny stories about castle life, they put on their tiny outfits and pretend they are kings and queens. They are so cute!

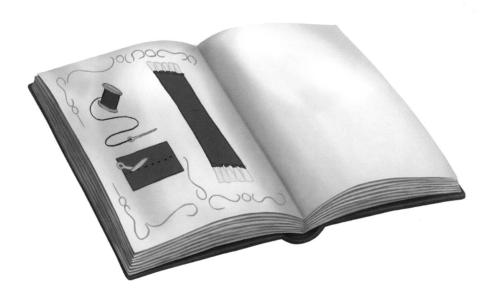

I love to sew, especially in the castle attic. Sometimes I open my mother's book of patterns and close my eyes, and whatever my finger lands on is the item I make. One day, my finger landed on a beautiful scarf. I knew just who to make it for: my loving Prince!

I searched deep inside my trunk and found the most beautiful royal blue fabric. Gus and Jaq brought me gold tassels from the bottom of a curtain someone had thrown away! They were as good as new to me.

The mice and I worked very hard on this
special gift. Suzy helped me sew. Gus and Jaq
smoothed the wrinkles out with their tiny hands.

Finally, the scarf was done. We all agreed it was the handsomest scarf we had ever seen—almost as handsome as my Prince!

When I gave the Prince his
gift, he smiled and kissed me.
He wore his new scarf as
proudly as he wears his crown.
It looked perfect on him! Suzy,
Gus, and Jaq clapped with glee.

I am very good at keeping my attic room a
secret. My love for the Prince is much harder
to hide!